My
Friend
the
Painter

Lygia Bojunga Nunes

My
Friend
the
Painter

Translated by Giovanni Pontiero

Harcourt Brace Jovanovich, Publishers

San Diego / New York / London

O Meu Amigo Pintor printed in Brazil
by Livraria Jose Olympio Editora S.A., 1987

Library of Congress Cataloging-in-Publication Data
Nunes, Lygia Bojunga, 1932–
[Meu amigo pintor. English]
My friend the painter/Lygia Bojunga Nunes;
translated by Giovanni Pontiero.
p. cm.
Translation of: O meu amigo pintor.
Summary: A young boy becomes friends with
the artist in the apartment upstairs and tries hard
to understand when his friend commits suicide.
ISBN 0-15-256340-7
[1. Artists — Fiction. 2. Suicide — Fiction.
3. Friendship — Fiction. 4. Brazil — Fiction.] I. Title.
PZ7.N9643My 1991
[Fic] — dc20 90-46043

Designed by Camilla Filancia
Printed in the United States of America
First edition A B C D E

To
Peter

Friday

I'M NOT SURE if I was born like this or if I became like this because of my friend the painter, but when I look at something, the first thing I notice is the color.

People, houses, books—it's always the same. The first thing I look at is the color of their eyes, of the doors, and of the covers of the books; only then do I begin to see what the rest is like.

One day my friend told me that I was a boy with the soul of an artist, and he gave me an album with some pictures he had done in water-colors, oil paints, and pastels. He said that he had arranged the pictures in an album to help me to understand better this question of color. On the first pages there is nothing but color. In fact, to begin with there isn't even color, only black and white. Then the colors begin: yellow, blue, red, and then lots of other colors as those three colors are mixed, in designs I sometimes like and sometimes don't like at all.

My friend told me that the more you look at a color, the more you get out of it. I sat there staring at him without understanding. I couldn't grasp what he meant about *getting so much out of a color*.

But today there was a moment when I wasn't in the mood for seeing anyone. So I opened the album he had given me. I just wanted to sit there studying the colors one by one, that's all. I looked and looked, as I had been told. And suddenly I knew exactly what he had been trying to tell me. I felt like going straight up to his apartment and saying to him: I've understood what you told me that day! I know just what you mean about this black. Believe me, I've got it and I can now see how this yellow took over.

But I couldn't speak to my friend the painter; he's dead. He died three days ago.

MY FRIEND LIVES—that is, he used to live—in the apartment above mine. I often went there to play backgammon with him; we would chat, and he had a clock on the wall that chimed on the hour and on the half hour. My father and mother used to grumble, "Ah, that insufferable chiming" and my sister would ask me, "Is there no hope of that friend of yours ever forgetting to wind his clock?"

But we all have our likes and dislikes, and I loved to hear the clock chiming. Especially at night.

Not just because it chimed so nicely.

Nor just because I think it's great to hear the hours striking.

It was because whenever the clock struck, I thought, my friend's up there.

For me, listening to the clock striking was

just like listening to my friend walking. Or talking. Or laughing. Do you know what I mean? For he was a very quiet man who only liked doing things that don't make a noise: smoking a pipe, thinking, and painting. Were it not for the clock chiming, you would almost have thought that he didn't live there.

But that's not what I wanted to tell you. What I wanted to tell you was that on Tuesday when I got home from school and went up to his apartment, he was dead. I couldn't look at him lying there dead. I turned to the wall and found myself facing a picture he had painted: a yellow woman. (He once told me that she was all yellow like this because she had woken up feeling happy, and still not knowing very much about colors, I thought this was just a painter having crazy ideas.)

I couldn't stay up there. I rushed back to my room.

Suddenly I began to feel all dark inside. So dark that I couldn't see anything else inside myself.

Then the clock began to strike. It chimed and chimed. For it was midday. And if anyone wants to know what color the chiming was, I can tell them at once. It was yellow! I had become just like my friend the painter: I was starting to find yellow a happy color. And it was so nice to hear the clock striking midday! Each stroke of the clock gave the impression that everyone was wrong and that my friend was still living upstairs.

And then my cousin had a birthday party. But I didn't go.

There was a soccer match at school. But I stayed home.

I was in the middle of reading a good book. But I didn't feel like reading anymore.

All I wanted to do was to stay in my room. Listening to the clock chiming upstairs.

And how it chimed. To begin with it was bright yellow. But then the yellow turned pale—got paler and paler. The clock started to wind down and this slowed down the chimes so that yellow became sadder and sadder, became whiter and whiter.

Today everything finally turned white: the clock stopped chiming. How I longed . . . oh, how I longed to go upstairs and wind it.

The door was locked.

"Who has the key?"

"That Clarice has it."

"But the clock needs winding."

"She's gone off with the key."

"But the clock . . ."

"She said she'd be back."

"But what about the clock?"

That night, when I went to bed, I lay awake, waiting, waiting, waiting.

Nothing. Nothing except all that white. I never thought that silence could be so white. And then, yes, I saw that my friend had really died and that white is more painful than black—*much* more painful than yellow! For white is more painful than any other color.

Monday

FOR ME, red is the color of something I'd like to understand.

Once (that was the year before last, just before my ninth birthday) my cousin came here with a friend called Janaína who was dressed all in red. Her dress had full sleeves and was much longer than the dresses worn by my sister and cousin, and there was no other color—just that bright red which made everyone in the room begin to stare. And on her forehead, like a tennis player, Janaína wore a red band, which matched her dress.

I fell in love with her.

And that night at dinner I said, "I love Janaína."

Everybody thought I was joking, and my sister said that Janaína was fifteen years old.

"So what? Why can't I fall in love with an older woman?"

"Just fancy that!" and everyone laughed.

I thought it was better to say no more. But I went on loving her. I mean, I *think* it was love; I couldn't be sure, but whenever I thought about Janaína (and I thought about her all the time) I felt something different inside me that I didn't understand, but it was red because, clearly, I could only think of Janaína dressed all in red.

One day, my cousin came again to Petrópolis with Janaína. My heart leaped when I heard my mother saying, "Hello, Janaína."

I ran into the sitting room. I couldn't believe it. There was Janaína wearing blue pants with a white blouse! And on her brow, instead of a headband, she had bangs.

The more I looked at Janaína the less I loved

her. When she left, I went upstairs and told my Friend the Painter (I think it's better to write it with a capital *F* and a capital *P*) everything that happened. He lit his pipe, stood looking out of the window as if he would stay there looking forever, and then he spoke. "Red is really a complicated color."

And nothing else. For he was like that: he didn't like talking if he wasn't in the mood. But when he was in the mood, the thing he loved to talk about was art. Between one game of backgammon and another (he once told my mother that playing backgammon with me was good for his head), he'd show me his portfolio of paintings, tell me about being an artist, and often I couldn't make heads or tails of the paintings he was showing me.

"But did you like it?" he would ask.

"Of course."

"Well, that's all that matters. One day you'll understand. Or you won't."

At such moments, I looked at my Friend and it wasn't only the paintings he was showing me that I didn't understand. I didn't understand him either.

I suppose that's why I spend so much time looking at the red he painted here in the album. To see if I can understand.

To see if I can understand.

To see if I can understand why there are people who kill themselves.

IT WAS ONLY after the clock stopped chiming and all that white remained up above, where my Friend used to live, it was only after I had cried a lot as I watched his corpse being carried out of the building and heard my mother saying that children don't have to go to funerals as she left me behind, that a girl who lives on the first floor came up to me and said, "Your Friend the Painter has gone to hell."

I got such a fright that I couldn't speak.

"He killed himself," she went on. "And people who kill themselves go straight to hell."

My speech came back. "Who says he killed himself?"

"Everybody's talking. He left a letter."

"Where is the letter?"

"I haven't got it."

"Who's got it then?"

"A friend of his, the one who used to come here."

"Dona Clarice?"

"Yes, that's her."

"And what does he explain in the letter?"

The girl just shrugged her shoulders and said with the expression of someone who isn't the least bit interested, "He must have roasted in hell by now like that chicken my mother forgot to take out of the oven."

I gave the horrid little girl one mighty shove and ran off.

BUT TODAY, unexpectedly, something happened which changed the kind of red I was feeling inside. By chance, I bumped into Dona Clarice as the elevator door opened. She was coming out as I was going in. I felt so confused that instead of saying hello, I asked her, "Does he explain in the letter why he killed himself?"

I never thought anyone could come out with such a horrible question without having time to hold it back. But out it came. And Dona Clarice stood still, holding the elevator door open, staring at me with wide eyes.

I felt so ashamed that I wanted to disappear.

Luckily, someone rang for the elevator. Dona Clarice, as if waking up, let go of the door and nervously touched her forehead. Suddenly, she appeared to remember something and held out a parcel she was carrying under her arm. My Friend the Painter had written on the wrapping: "For my playmate."

"I was going to ask the porter to give you this,"

she said. She stood there, looking down at the floor, then said in a whisper, "No, he didn't kill himself. He died just as . . . just as everybody dies one day." And she said good-bye and rushed off.

I stood there staring at my Friend's writing on the parcel. Then I remembered the clock and went racing after her. If she had the key to his apartment, she could come back and wind the clock.

But she had already vanished down the street.

I opened the parcel. It was the backgammon board (it folds in the middle and closes like a box for storing the pieces and dice).

I was so pleased that my Friend had left me the board. But I was even more pleased with what Dona Clarice had told me while looking down at the floor.

FOR ME, my Friend's death is also something red, something difficult to understand. But if it came as it does to so many people every day, then it's much easier to begin to understand.

So I went back home with those words going through my head: he died just as everybody dies one day. And then something happened: yellow began to appear there inside my red.

Tuesday

TODAY I WAS GETTING out of the bath when I heard the caretaker arrive (he's the father of the daughter of that mother who forgot the chicken in the oven); I ran like lightning to my bedroom and shut the door. Not because I didn't want him to see me naked—no, it wasn't that—but, to be honest, I can't stand him.

He once said that a painter only paints a woman yellow because he doesn't know how to paint her as she really looks. The type of man who knows nothing about art, don't you think?

Another time, I was upstairs playing back-gammon with my Friend when the bell rang. When I opened the door there were two men who said they were policemen. They told me to run off home: they wanted to be alone with my Friend to ask him a few questions. Later, we discovered it was the caretaker who had gone to the police to inform them that my Friend was living here in the building.

Trust him to go poking his nose into other people's business.

Besides, every time this caretaker comes to our apartment, it's either to complain about somebody in the building, or to drag my father and mother off to a meeting of the neighbors (which they detest).

So I thought it better to stay quietly here in my room.

But after a while I heard my Friend's name being mentioned and I started listening to the conversation in the sitting room. I had to open the door to hear what my father was saying. He was talking about suicide, and every time he and my mother spoke the word *suicide* they lowered their voices. But not the caretaker; he has a voice like a foghorn. Even when he whispers you can hear him from the far end of the street. And there he was, whispering that my Friend had been singled out because of his political views (I couldn't understand what that meant), and—who knows?—perhaps that is why my Friend killed himself.

"Did he think he was going to be arrested again?" my mother asked.

And that set them off: politics here, politics there.

I couldn't keep quiet any longer. I went into the sitting room and told them, "Dona Clarice said that my Friend died just as everybody dies one day. He didn't do it on purpose!"

"Isn't that what you would expect her to say?" the caretaker said.

Looking at my father, I replied, "She knew him better than anyone, and she assured me he didn't do it on purpose."

"What else could she say," that loud voice went on, "so that nobody would think he killed himself because of her?"

I kept on looking at my father, and my father kept on looking at me.

"But why would he do that?" I asked.

"He was sick, my boy."

"Sick? We were playing backgammon the night before. Three games. One after the other. And there was nothing wrong with him!"

"Sick *up here*." My father tapped his forehead. "Only someone who is very sick does what he did."

"Please, won't you tell me exactly what happened?"

Here my mother said that they were already late for their meeting. I got excited. "But he was my Friend!"

The caretaker got to his feet. "Isn't it time we went?"

"A friend for life! He himself told me that age doesn't matter when it comes to being a sincere friend. And you think I'm not going to find out if he really did it on purpose?"

My mother put her arms around me. "You must stop thinking about it, Claudio. At your age you should be thinking about life and not death. You have other friends—"

"But I don't like any of them as much as I liked him!"

"—you have lots of things to study, to play with, to invent. Stop thinking about what happened to him and get on with your own life, my boy!"

And off she went, while I stayed behind, left hanging in midair. I went back to my room. I thought my father was probably being more truthful than Dona Clarice. Not because he is my father—no, that wasn't the reason—but he had looked me straight in the eye while Dona Clarice had kept staring at the floor.

But I can't be sure. I can't stop thinking: Did he really take his own life? And if he did, why did he do it?

He enjoyed his painting, playing backgammon, eating and thinking; he loved listening to the clock chiming; and if he saw a flower down below he would lean out of the window and say, "See how pretty it is."

Was he going to put an end to all that which was so good?

If he had fallen out of the window when leaning over to look at the flower, if he had choked on his food and suffocated, or if he had turned into an old man—but to go like this? Deciding for himself? Saying, I'm going to finish myself off right now?!

Why, why, *why?*

The backgammon board was open (this was our day for playing), and the album he had given me was also open at a watercolor showing a yellow boat sinking into a sea the color of . . . what was that color?

It wasn't beige.

It wasn't light brown.

It could almost have been that color my Friend

liked and called burnt sienna. But it wasn't that either.

It wasn't pink or orange, so what was it?

There and then, I decided that it was the color-of-longing, and that was that.

On the opposite page, just to show how colors change, my Friend had painted another watercolor. After sinking into that sea with its color-of-longing, the boat reappears, but after that dip, the yellow has become different, strange, the kind of yellow I don't like at all and which I almost feel like calling caretaker-yellow.

The more I looked at that boat, the more I believed Dona Clarice had lied to me. And the more I believed it, the more that yellow reminded me of the caretaker's face, and the more I felt like the boat: surrounded by the color-of-longing.

A color-of-longing that was even starting to turn red as I tried hard to understand.

So Dona Clarice had lied to me. But *why?*

So my Friend really had died on purpose. But *why?*

And why should people make such a mystery of suicide? And start whispering? Giving the impression that suicide is an ugly word—*why?*

If a man is arrested for stealing or murder, boys my age always get to know about it. So if they say "he's a political prisoner," why do people my age never know exactly what that means— *why?*

And the more that *why* appeared, the more that caretaker-yellow remained, and the stronger that color-of-longing became.

BESIDES, with all that white of the clock that no longer chimes, and with that backgammon board looking at me as if to remind me that this was our day for playing, I'm obviously going to miss him more and more. And if this longing keeps growing like this, who knows what will happen?

Thursday

IN MY ALBUM there's a painting that is all the color-of-longing, and in front there are three people: one in white and two in blue. Their faces are half-faded, and I've often wondered if the faces are of men or women.

For I wanted to know what my Friend was thinking when he painted those three figures. I wanted to know so I could compare, because last night I dreamed about them. But I overslept and raced out of the house. We're producing a play at school, and I had a rehearsal this morning.*

* After agreeing to take part in the play I regretted it. I don't want to become an actor because I'm rather shy; the thing I really want to be is a painter.

31

And once the rehearsal was over, I had forgotten the dream. I could only remember the colors and the three figures, but I couldn't remember what had happened.

Dreams are so strange; you wake up with all those things that happened inside you and then, in a flash, you've forgotten.

I decided to wait and see if anything came back to me. But I couldn't remember a thing.

I tried so hard to remember last night that I dreamed once again about the same color and the same three figures. Now I don't know whether or not it was the same dream all over again.

Never mind. Let me tell you at once about the second dream before that goes out of my head as well.

THE STAGE CURTAIN was the color-of-longing. I was sitting in the theater looking at it, and when the curtain went up, the stage was empty. There was no scenery, no props, not even a chair or anything.

But the entire stage was the same color as the curtain and everyone sitting in the theater found themselves looking at all that longing and nothing else.

The clock began to chime nicely.

I counted twelve strokes.

I couldn't tell whether it was midday or midnight: the color wasn't any more like night than day.

After the clock stopped chiming, the three figures came onstage. They were all the same height, and the three of them entered shoulder to shoulder, one in white, two in blue. And the moment I looked at the figure in white, I recognized my Friend the Painter who was playing the part of a ghost. And do you know something? I was really scared.

As for the other two figures, I couldn't tell what parts they were supposed to be playing. But their blue costumes were so bright that they lit up the stage and made the color-of-longing all the stronger. And stronger inside me, too.

Seeing my Friend turned into a ghost, and feeling and seeing that strong color-of-longing, I couldn't stand it any longer. I burst into tears.

I sobbed my heart out.

Everyone in the audience began to whisper.

"Hush!"

"Hush!"

"Hussssssssssh."

And my sobs got louder and louder. What a fool I made of myself.

My Friend stood still on stage. He and the other two figures. They neither moved nor said a word.

The audience became impatient and started clapping, stamping, and whistling. And nothing was happening onstage.

I began to find the whole thing so odd that I stopped weeping. I looked at my Friend. He took his hand from his pocket (I was sitting right at the back, but I could see that it was his hand all right: it was stained with paint and holding a paintbrush), and he waved to me with his brush.

The audience stopped stamping their feet and whistling; people were staring at me. I got up and made my way to the stage. My legs were shaking so much that I could hardly walk. I don't know whether it was the embarrassment of seeing all those people staring at me or whether it was the fear of getting so close to my Friend now that he had turned into a ghost. But I got there. And he whispered in my ear:

"And now, Claudio?"

"Now, what?"

"I don't know how to play the part of a ghost, so what am I going to do? I don't know what I'm supposed to say."

My heart was in my mouth. I asked him in the tiniest whisper, "But haven't you rehearsed the play?"

He shook his head.

"Haven't you learned your lines?"

"There wasn't time. They put me into this costume, pushed me onto the stage, told me 'You're a ghost,' and that was that."

"Oh!"

Once more the audience began stamping their feet loudly.

"Tell them to start acting," I whispered.

"Who?"

"Those two standing beside you."

"I've already told them. They say they're supposed to be the chorus."

"They're what?"

"They're supposed to comment as I tell my story. But if I don't tell my story, they can't comment on anything."

"What a mess!"

"And now, Claudio? What am I going to say? What am I going to do? Look, they're all waiting—they're starting to boo."

"Get off! Tell them you don't want to be a ghost."

"I can't."

"Why not?"

"I'm caught: my costume is sewn to theirs."

I went behind my Friend to see if I could detach the white from the blue without anyone noticing. Some hope.

"It's not thread!" I said. "It's paint."

"Then it's hopeless trying to separate us."

The audience was in an uproar; some were shouting, "What's going on here? When are we going to see some acting?"

I felt so nervous that I began sobbing again. My Friend started to panic.

"This is no time to be crying—you've got to help me! Help me, help me!"

I had to invent something to save my Friend. Taking a deep breath as if I were about to take a deep dive, I went up to the footlights and began to sing the national anthem.

The audience stopped booing. Everyone joined in the singing. This gave me time to think about what I was going to say.

The anthem came to an end. The audience applauded. I spoke:

"Ladies and gentlemen: Your attention, please. I'm going to tell you the story about this ghost. It's a short story because he died recently. Let me tell you why he turned into a ghost. He made a mistake about his time for dying. I never thought such a thing could happen. But it did. He should have lived to a ripe old age, but he was an artist; he was a painter (you only have to look at the brush in his hand); he had this passion for colors. He would wake up in the morning and instead of saying like everybody else, 'I'm sad' or 'I'm happy,' he would say, 'Today I'm purple.'

" 'Today I've become so yellow!'

" 'Today I woke up almost purple, but I started turning yellow in the evening.'

"For him, the thing that looked most like the color-of-death was mist. Sometimes, when the sky was blue in the morning but became misty in the afternoon, he would say, 'This morning there was life in the air but it now looks as if it wants to die.'

"And then, one day, there was the heaviest mist you ever saw. The Painter looked out of his window and all he could see was that mist covering everything that is color, and he said, as he was in the habit of saying, 'It looks as if life wants to die.'

"Mist as heavy as that usually clears up quickly, but that time it didn't. It lasted all afternoon and all through the night. The Painter kept looking out of the window and there seemed to be no end to that wish of dying. That's why he got it wrong. He thought the mist would never go away and so he decided to kill the wish.

"What a mistake! Next morning, day broke with the prettiest blue sky.

"But the Painter had already turned into a ghost."

As I got to the end of my story about the ghost

I turned to the nearest of the two figures in blue and whispered, "Right, there's the story. Make your comment. Speak. Say something."

What's the use! Both of them looked at me angrily and the one dressed in the brighter blue muttered, "We're not like him, you know: we've learned our parts; we've rehearsed the play; we know what we have to say line by line."

"Well, say them then!"

"But what we've memorized has nothing to do with the story you've told!" And they just stood there as glum and silent as could be.

The audience began protesting again.

One man got up and asked, "Would you like to explain what those actors think they're doing standing up there like dummies without saying anything?"

That gave me an idea, and I replied, "They're performing a *tableau*. That's what it is! Surely you must have guessed by now? They've come here to show a picture by that Painter. And you look at pictures, you don't listen to them."

And just as I was beginning to sigh with relief, the tiresome fellow asked me, "Then why did you tell the story about the ghost?"

I had no more ideas. I didn't know what to say.

My Friend whispered, "Tell him it's because the mist is thick outside and you want them to be careful not to make the same mistake as I did."

"It's because the mist is thick outside and so that you don't make the same mistake as I did, I mean, as he did."

And at that moment I woke up.

Besides, with that fellow going on at me and everyone staring, I couldn't stand it any longer.

Saturday

I HAVE A CLASSMATE, you know, and we're friends. Only he's not a friend forever like my Friend the Painter (there are days when I wonder if you can have more than one friend for life), and yesterday on the playground we talked about hearts.

It all started because I was drawing a heart, only instead of the heart being red, it was brown; and instead of being like the heart we all know, it was flattened on one side and suddenly broke off, leaving you wondering what happened to it.

When I finished the drawing I showed it to my friend.

"What's that?" he asked.

"Can't you see?"

"See what?"

"Can't you see what it is?"

"No."

"Well, take a guess."

"How am I supposed to know?"

"It's my heart."

He looked and looked.

"You still can't see it?" I asked him.

"No, I can't! For a start, hearts are red."

"Okay, but this is *my* heart."

"So what? Because it's yours, it's not red?"

"It's not that. It's because I'm bothered that my heart's like this, looking as if it had taken a punch and been flattened on one side."

"A punch!"

"Besides, a red heart is common. Mine's not common: it's quite different, so it has to be another color. Well, does it or doesn't it?"

My friend looked at the paper, then looked at me.

"It can't be. It must be red. And it should be

pointed at the bottom. Give me the paper and I'll show you what it's like."

"Wait a minute! You don't understand. It's just that . . ."

"Give me the paper; let me draw it properly."

"Do me a favor and listen to what I'm telling you. If my heart's different, feels poorly, and is fed up, I'm not going to draw it like that heart everybody draws for their girlfriend, am I? Wait a minute! Stop pulling!"

But he pulled. And took a red pen from his pocket and began changing the color of my heart. And he made it pointed at the bottom, and said, "A heart must have an arrow!"

He stuck an arrow in the middle. Started correcting it on one side, then on the other, didn't leave my heart even the tiniest bit squashed, and, like a fool, I still tried to explain.

"But I told you that it got squashed with worry."

"Well, if it's squashed, speak up, friend," and he stuck another arrow higher up and wrote:

I'm squashed because I'm fed up. "Right! Now everybody understands." And he gave me back my heart.

That did it and I told him, "What do I want with that junk?" And he replied, "That drawing of yours was junk." And just then he saw Denise (a girl he thinks is great). He grabbed the drawing from my hand and where he had written *I'm fed up*, he put a colon and scrawled in big letters: YOU'RE NOT LOOKING AT ME!! He ran off, gave my heart to Denise, and went off to kick a ball about.

Ah.

So much the better.

What was I going to do with a heart that had nothing to do with mine?

I THINK IT WILL BE a long time before I find a friend who also understands this business about a heart getting squashed and turning brown.

Sunday

OF ALL THE THINGS I remember about my Friend, there are two I remember most. I don't know why.

The first is a conversation we had one Sunday. It was raining. We had just finished playing. My Friend got up, lit his pipe, began preparing some paints, and then talked about love.

The love of working. Of painting. The love of a man and woman, of a father, a mother, love for your city, your country, the world we live in, the love of a son, a friend.

"Love like the one we have for each other," he said.

My heart jumped.

I've always been fond of my Friend, but I always thought he was less fond of me. I don't know if it was because I'm a child and he wasn't, or if it was because he was an artist and I wasn't. I only know that when he spoke of *love* my heart jumped like that. Could it be, then, that we both liked each other exactly the same?

I wanted to see at once if it was true.

"How do you like me?"

"It depends. Sometimes I like you as a father. I'm sorry that you're not my son, that I can't say, 'I'm the one who made this marvelous boy!' " He smiled. Then he became serious, sat down before his easel, and began to paint. "But at other times, I've no desire to be your father. I only want to be your friend, that's all." He painted a little more. "Sometimes I like you because you're my playmate; at times because I wish I was you. In other words, to be a child again. So that's it: every day I like you in some way or other. And if you put them together, you'll see that I like you a lot. You'll see that it's love."

I was so pleased to hear him say that he loved me that I sat still without saying another word, simply watching him paint. But after a while, I couldn't resist asking, "Do you think we're alike?"

"Not in looks, but in other ways. Our way of keeping quiet, our way of sneezing without having a cold, our way of seeing things. I've had many a grown-up friend, but never anyone so like me as you."

"Yes, but with a grown-up friend you can talk about things you don't tell me."

"For example?"

I was itching to say that he didn't talk to me about Dona Clarice, but I thought I might annoy him. I simply shrugged my shoulders and kept on looking at his paintbrush. He was painting a corner of the room. A chair. A table. A lamp. But then he started to paint part of a woman's body. I say part for he decided to paint the woman right on the edge of the canvas.

I was so puzzled about that woman—you could see only one leg, a little bit of her dress, and not much hair (the rest of her disappeared out of the picture).

I know that a painter likes to paint things differently. And I had already learned that to be a good painter doesn't mean you have to paint everything just as you would see it in a photograph. So it wasn't because the woman disappeared out of the picture that I was puzzled. It was because, even with the little that appeared, she looked just like all the other women my Friend painted.

The room was full of pictures, which he went on painting and hanging up; many of them were of women. I looked at them one by one, just to be sure about what I was thinking. And I was right! The woman might be fat, thin, black, white; she could have an eye, a nose, and a mouth, or her face could be just a blob such as he liked to paint; but the woman always looked the same. And there was always a touch of yellow.

"Why do all the women you paint look the same?"

He kept on painting and took his time before replying, "There is a woman who lives in my thoughts, you know; I don't even notice when she goes out of my head and comes into my painting."

I asked without thinking, "Is it Dona Clarice?"

And he replied at once, "It is." But with that he stopped painting. He got up. Stood there looking at one picture, then another. He ended up saying, "But I didn't mean them always to turn out the same. The yellow, certainly, I put in on purpose. Yellow for me is also the color-of-Clarice, and I like to put a little of her into everything I paint."

"Just a little? Look at this one here: she's all yellow."

"That was actually Clarice (one happy day), but not these others. If I was a good painter, I'd have them all looking different, even though I'm always thinking about Clarice. I'd paint each of them as they are, not all looking alike."

"But you *are* a good painter!"

"No! No, I'm not. I know very well how one should paint; I have technique; I work and work to see if I can bring life to my paintings. But it's no good: my paintings are dead." He pointed with his brush. "Look! Look! Look! Can't you see? Can't you feel that my painting has no life?"

And with this, he threw his brush onto the table almost as if—how can I put it?—almost as if in despair. I'd never seen him like that before.

I KEEP ON REMEMBERING that day, and wondering if it's possible that an artist can love his work so much . . . let me see how I can explain this . . . love his work so much that if he finds his work has no life, he doesn't want to go on living either.

THE OTHER MEMORY that keeps coming into my head is of an excursion we made together soon after deciding that he would teach me how to paint.

It was sunny. I was still on holiday. We went out of the city, taking paints, brushes, and paper. We stopped near some woods. My mother had made sandwiches. On the ground there was fresh grass, very short. We sat down and ate (not the grass—the sandwiches).

All around, everything was green. My Friend then talked about green: strong, pale, green in every possible shade. He showed me his paints, showed me the grass. Comparing them. We painted. He lay on the ground. Looked up at the clouds. He slept, snored, dreamed. He woke up and said, "I was dreaming about Clarice." I was surprised to hear him speaking about her like this. He spoke as if he were dreaming, looking up at the sky, his arm behind him as if it were a cushion.

He told me how they fell in love. She was his first girl; he was her first boy. He was still in his teens. How they longed for time to pass quickly so that they could marry! It passed slowly. And they kept on waiting. Until one day, time had passed. But they didn't marry: they began to quarrel. She complained that all he cared about was politics, that instead of only loving her, he'd started caring about everyone, that instead of always being with her, he was forever going to political rallies and meetings—up north, down south—traveling all over Brazil until one day he even disappeared. They had arrested him.

"How does one get crazy about politics?" I asked. "Is it just like getting crazy about a girl?"

"It is and it isn't." And instead of explaining to me, he went on with what he was telling me and how he was in prison for a long time. "I always wrote to Clarice, but she never received my letters." And so she thought he had forgotten her. One day, tired of waiting, she married someone else. And she had a son. Only last year, they met each other again. Suddenly, just like that, they bumped into each other on the street. They stood there looking at each other and couldn't believe their eyes. Realizing that they still loved each other even though such a long time had passed—here my Friend closed his eyes and I thought that he had fallen asleep again.

I LIKE TO THINK about that day. It was so good to lie there near the edge of the woods, having that conversation man-to-man. I looked at my hand while he lay there with his eyes shut: it was covered with paint like his. I liked having my hand just like his. I lay there waiting. And he finished telling me the rest of the story.

"Afterwards, whenever Clarice came to visit me, I begged her to leave everything and stay with me. But she always said no. Do you know what she said? That I was a man torn between three passions: my passion for her, for painting, and for politics." He looked at me. "But it wasn't because of this that she didn't stay with me. No, I'm sure it was because of her son."

"But when I see some politician talking on television I find the whole business so complicated, so boring. How can you get passionate about politics?"

He sat up. Quietly lit his pipe. I also sat up to listen. But he finished by simply saying, "Politics is really a complicated affair."

And that's it. Just like the day I told him the story about Janaína's red dress. And with that he began teaching me again about the color green, and during the rest of our outing we only talked about paints, drawing boards, and brushes.

Monday

LAST NIGHT the three returned. Those same three figures from my dream.

I'm even beginning to wonder if from now on they will live in my sleep, and every time I want to dream, they will decide to visit me.

THE THREE ARRIVED as they did last time: joined together. But this time they were wearing green costumes. (A green just like the green smock my Friend wore for painting.) But in this dream, you know, instead of one being a ghost and the others the chorus, they were the three passions of my Painter Friend.

They said hello, sat down, and began to chat. All three had the same voice.

Everything the one said amused the others. And they all had the same laugh.

With all that sameness so divided between the three, I couldn't tell which was Dona Clarice, which was Painting, and which was Politics.

The more they laughed, the more they pressed up against each other. They appeared to be only one person sitting there on the sofa, which had a patterned cover.

Suddenly, I decided to ask if they were jealous of each other since my Friend liked all three of them at the same time.

One burst out laughing; the second got scared; but the third one put on the face of Dona Clarice and explained, "In the beginning I wanted him to love only me. I was jealous of that one." She pointed. "When he went on painting instead of loving me, I got hopping mad."

The second one looked at me and put on a

face as if to say, "How silly to be jealous of his work, don't you think?"

And the third one continued, "Not to mention that one!" She pointed to the first one. "I felt so terribly jealous when he began traveling north and south chasing after her, saying that he had important work to do."

The first one frowned.

"Instead of being jealous, you should have gone and worked with him for the good of Brazil."

"That's right."

At this all three sighed alike. And they appeared to be thinking alike as well, slumped on the sofa. But then they straightened up, and Dona Clarice spoke.

"Yes, but that was ages ago. Then I saw there was no point in expecting him to love just me."

"It was almost as if he was so tiny inside that there was only room for one love, was it not?" the second one said.

And the first one piped up, "That's right."

"And then: *hey presto!* my jealousy disappeared."

"*Hey presto!*"

"*Hey presto!*"

And every time one of them said *hey presto*, they hugged each other. It was so funny! I burst out laughing. But they looked very serious and said, "Now that we're buddies and gathered together inside him, your Friend can live in peace."

"And let me tell you: he's going to be happy— happy forever!"

I was so pleased with this news that I squeezed myself onto the sofa to be closer to them. But then they said:

"We can't stay—we must get on with loving."

"And working."

"And politics."

They got up, saying good-bye with one voice; and no sooner had they left than my dream

found that it had become very empty, and—
hey presto!—it was over.

WHAT A SHAME! It was so nice sitting there, knowing that my Friend was going to be happy.

Monday
Afternoon

As i was coming back from school, Rosalia said that my Friend's girlfriend was there.

Rosalia is the daughter of the caretaker; the girlfriend is Dona Clarice; and *there* was the apartment of my Friend the Painter.

I said, "Oh, is she?" with the expression of someone who's paying no attention, but my heart was jumping. I saw at once that I had to speak to Dona Clarice and to ask her what I kept wanting to know.

I rushed into the elevator, quickly practicing in my head what I should say to her. I had to be quick because the elevator soon arrived and I didn't want to be standing there shyly in front of my Friend's door without pressing the bell or anything. I pressed. Dona Clarice was slow in opening the door, and that gave me time to practice some more.

She opened the door; I opened my mouth; and the clock chimed. Having rehearsed my speech so carefully, I was at a loss for words.

It's incredible how that chime (only one, it was on the half hour) left me like this . . . don't ask me why. At first I was pleased; the clock chiming was certainly the sound of my Friend. It seemed almost as if he had come back. But suddenly I thought of him as I had seen him on that last day: dead forever. And that chime of the clock went on striking inside me in such a red manner, so difficult to understand that—how could I remember what I was supposed to say? Besides, Dona Clarice was standing there watching me and wearing the brightest color-of-longing.

I looked at her dress and inside the room. At her dress and at the clock. At her dress and at the chair my Friend used to sit in.

Then she asked, "Won't you come in?"

"No. I only wanted to know why you lied to me." (All very different from what I'd rehearsed!)

We looked at each other.

I explained, "It's just that—you said that he died like everybody dies one day. But everybody doesn't decide to die on purpose, do they?"

"Won't you come in?"

I went in for a minute. And as she still didn't speak I ended up saying, "I *need* to know what really happened to him."

"Why do you say I lied?"

"Then you didn't lie? Then the news hasn't gone around, and the whole world doesn't know that he killed himself?"

She moved to the far end of the room. Stopped beside the window. Stood there looking out. How strange, my Friend also used to think like this, on his feet, as if he were looking onto the street.

When I thought she was never going to answer me, I asked, "Was it because you think I'm a child? At home they think this isn't something you discuss with children." She looked at me. "Do you also believe that? Is that why you lied to me?"

"No. I have a son your age and I discuss everything with him."

"And what about suicide? Do you discuss that, too?"

She nodded.

"Did you tell him that my . . . that your . . . that our Friend . . ."

"I told him."

"Then why didn't you tell me?"

She turned to face the window. And when she kept her back to me and said nothing more, I ended up blurting out, "So that I don't think like everyone else that it was because of you that he did it?"

She looked at me quickly and I was like this . . . How can I explain it? Half ashamed and half angry. To be frank, I still feel a bit angry all the time. Ever since the caretaker arrived at our house and started that rumor that it was because of her . . .

"What do you mean?" she asked. "Do they believe all this happened because of me?"

"They do."

"And do you believe it?"

I remained silent (wasn't she also silent?) looking at the pictures my Friend had painted.

She came up to me and looked deep into my eyes. "I don't know why he did it. I thought he looked sad; one day I asked him if he was like that because of politics or because of his work. It was then that he told me that he would never be a great painter: the more he worked the more he saw how difficult it was to express on canvas what he wanted to say. You, who were also his friend, didn't you also find him sad?"

I started to think. Yes, sometimes I did. Other times I thought it wasn't sadness: it was only that quiet way of his.

She didn't wait for me to reply; she continued, "He wanted me to leave my family and marry him. But I didn't have the courage. And so we agreed to wait. I think about all those things, but I still don't know why he did it." At this point I thought she was going to cry. But she said, "We were like this"—she joined two fingers. "The last time I was with him, we agreed on a number of things: a film we wanted to see, a trip we wanted to take. We agreed to remain like this forever." Once more she joined two fingers, and I noticed that her hand was trembling; her voice, too, was all shaky and getting lower and lower. "When I returned, he had killed himself. In the letter he left for me he simply painted a bunch of flowers. Daisies and carnations, which he knew I liked. And below, instead of an explanation, there was only a message begging forgiveness; something so strange, so short . . . simply saying: 'Can you forgive me?' Nothing else."

She returned to the window and stood with her back to me.

I remained still just like her. So my Friend decided to go away from life like this without explaining why, even to her? Let people think what they like—end of story?

I couldn't stay there any longer looking at the pictures he had painted, the chair in which he had sat, the clock that was just about to strike again and hurt me. "Bye," I said. And I began to leave without even remembering what I had asked. But she called my name.

"Claudio!" And she came close to me. "I know how much you loved him. When you love someone like this it's very difficult to live with a memory you don't understand. Like the one I'm living with now. That's why I lied that day. I thought my lie might stick, so that every time you remembered him you wouldn't be asking why? why?? why! Just as I'm always asking."

We hugged each other and I went away.

Sunday

THE WHOLE WEEK passed in a way I didn't
like one little bit. Every time I remembered my
Friend that *why? why?* came with him. Such an
awful thought!

And to make matters worse, the weather was
horrible. Rain, rain. Rain and that fog so you
can't see anything when you look out of the window, and they say that the only fog worse than
that of Petrópolis is in England. So I was really
in the dumps. I thought that the rain was never
going to end and that I would never be able to
remember my Friend without finding it so awful.

Then on Thursday morning in school, I was

looking at my notebook and thought to myself:
These two pages are stuck so close together! But
it's easy to separate them: you only have to pull.
And I pulled. The page came away. I hid it at
the back of the notebook. Then I attached it again
to the other one. I separated it. I attached it. I
separated it. I played. I attached it. And suddenly
I wanted to try doing the same thing with the
memory of my Friend: to separate *Friend* here
and *why?* there.

I tried. I only had to think:

Why did he want to die like this, on purpose?

Why did he explain nothing in his letter?

Why was he arrested?

Why didn't he tell me what he was going to
do?

Why did he want to put life into what he
painted but couldn't?

And each *why* that came into my head attached to my Friend I tried to pull out, to tear
out, to bury right down inside my skull.

I tried for two days. Even going along the street I went: one—two, one—two, one—two.

One was Friend.

Two was Why?

One was Think!

Two was Hide!

Think! Hide!

Think! Hide!

Think! Something broke down in my head, I tell you. Yesterday it even sounded a bit like an engine when you switch it on and it doesn't start.

BUT TODAY, when I woke up, there was an unbelievable blue coming through my window. And there was the nicest sunshine, so yellow that when I tried to look straight at it began to turn orange.

I remembered the picture my Friend had painted at the end of the album: that also has a summer sky.

I opened the album to compare the blue that he had painted with the blue I was seeing.

My Friend had joined up the two last pages of the album to be able to paint that broad sky.

I stayed there looking and looking at the way he had joined up those two pages. I looked so much that I ended up knowing that there was no need to separate *Friend* here and *why* there. What I had to do was what he did with the pages and the blue of the sky—join them up. Close together.

AND SO I put them together.

NOW WHEN I THINK of my Friend (and I still think about him a lot), I think of all of him. That's to say: pipe, paint, *why?*, backgammon, how he liked to look at flowers, his death on purpose, *why?*, the clock chiming, yellow, *why?*, green smock; everything joined together and mixed up.

And I am beginning to enjoy thinking like this.

I even believe that if I go on liking each *why* that appears, I'll end up understanding them one by one.